A Pipkin of Pepper

A PIPKIN OF PEPPER
A PICTURE CORGI BOOK: 978 0 552 54631 7

First published in Great Britain by Doubleday,
an imprint of Random House Children's Publishers UK

Doubleday edition published 2004
Picture Corgi edition published 2005

12

Copyright © Helen Cooper, 2004
Designed by Ian Butterworth

Set in Cochin

Picture Corgi books are published by Random House Children's Publishers UK,
61–63 Uxbridge Road, London W5 5SA,
a division of The Random House Group Ltd,
Addresses for companies within The Random House Group Limited can
be found at:www.randomhouse.co.uk/offices.htm
Isle of Houghton, Corner Boundary Road & Carse O'Gowrie, Houghton 2198, South Africa

The RANDOM HOUSE GROUP Limited Reg.No. 954009
www.randomhousechildrens.co.uk
www.wormworks.com

A CIP catalogue record for this book is available from the British Library

Printed in China

FOR
ANNIE EATON

A Pipkin of Pepper

Helen Cooper

Picture
Corgi

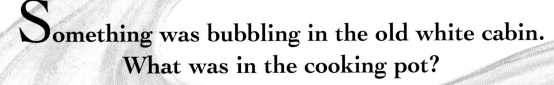

Something was bubbling in the old white cabin.
What was in the cooking pot?

Pumpkin Soup!

Made by a Cat, a Squirrel and a Duck,
waiting just for a pipkin of salt
to make it the best you ever tasted . . .

but . . .

"No salt left!" quacked the Duck.
They'd run *clean* out,
it was true.
There wasn't a grain, not a speckle of salt,
to put into the Pumpkin Soup!
Would it still taste good?

NO!

The Cat said, "I'm going shopping."

"Oh, please," begged the Duck. "Let me come too."

But the Duck hadn't been to the City before,
and he had a habit of wandering off.

"What if you get lost?" the Cat mewed.
"I won't!" squawked the Duck. "And if I do, I'll tell a Policedog."

"You'll never find a Policedog!"
yelled the Cat.

"If you're ever lost," said the Squirrel,
"the best thing to do
is stay where you are, and we'll find you."

It was time to catch the bus.

"Can I go?" pleaded Duck. "Can I go?" he said,

and he wiggled,

and wheedled,

and bobbed,

and begged,

until the Cat said, "**All right!**

If you promise to hold on tight."

"And I'll come too,"
said the Squirrel,
"and hold on to you."

But the Duck felt scared
when he first saw the City.
It was very big,
and very busy.
He stared at the stores,
and the towers,
and quacked,
"Let's buy that salt
and go straight back."

"Hold on tight," said the Squirrel.
"The salt shop isn't far from here."

And the Cat led them past
more towers,
and more stores,
selling allsorts.
Puddings and pastries,
pilchards and prawns,
lobsters and light bulbs,
pizza . . .

. . . and pepper . . .

And that gave Duck a clever idea.

"Wouldn't it be fine," he murmured,
"if we bought some pepper
for the Pumpkin Soup.

I bet it would taste . . .

". . . delicious!"
he quacked.
"Can we buy some?"

"Pepper?" squeaked the Squirrel.
"We won't need that."

"There's the salt shop," said the Cat.
"We have a job to do, and we don't
want to miss the bus back."

The PEPPER POT

Muntok White
Malabar Pepper
Pink Pepper
Green Pepper
Royal Pepper
Cracked Pepper
Black Pepper
Red Pepper
Chili Pepper
Sweet Pepper
Hawaiian Rainbow Pepper
Cayenne Pepper
Jalapeño Pepper
White Pepper
Pimento

A PIPKIN OF PEPPER FOR THE PUMPKIN SOUP!

But the Duck wasn't even listening.
He was thinking about pepper, for the Pumpkin Soup.
"Would one pipkin be quite enough?" he turned round to ask . . .

. . . but . . .

. . . the others had gone!

"Lost!"

quacked the Duck.
"I'm lost in the City!"
He scuttled off, in a terrible tizzy.

I nside the salt shop,
the Cat and the Squirrel
were busily buying
a small bag of salt.
They didn't even notice
that Duck was missing,
until the salt
was paid for and packed.

"Where can he be?" howled the Cat.
And the Squirrel wailed,
"Where did we see him last?"

"At the pepper shop!"
they shouted together.

They hurried back.

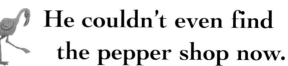But poor Duck
was lost in the crowd.
He couldn't even find
the pepper shop now.
He collided with a kind Mother Hen.

"Are you lost?" she clucked.

"Yes!" bawled the Duck.
"And I can't find my friends."

"Where did you see them last?" asked the Hen.

"At the pepper shop," sniffed the Duck.
"And I should have waited there
till they came back . . .

. . . but I forgot."

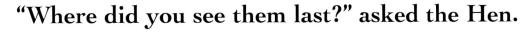

"I know the shop," said the Hen.
"And the Pepperdog might have
seen your friends.
Let's go and ask him."

I HOPE CAT AND SQUIRREL STAY IN ONE PLACE

"A Cat and a Squirrel?" said the Pepperdog.
"They just left by the other door."

"I'll never see them again!"
wailed the Duck.

And nothing would cheer him up.

WAAAA
WAA WA WA WAA

Not even a drink,

WA WA WA WAA

not even a snack,

WA?

not even a packet of pepper.

HE
LIKES
THAT
PEPPER

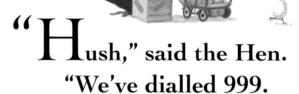

"Hush," said the Hen.
"We've dialled 999.
Any minute now, they'll come right through that door."
Pretty soon . . . through that door . . .
. . . came:

six Policedogs, with megaphones,

four helpful Firedogs,

two Foxes . . .   who left rather quickly.

And . . .

AT LAST . . .

. . . the Squirrel and Cat. The Duck was so pleased to see them.
The Cat wasn't cross, and the Squirrel didn't scold.
Even though they'd missed the last bus.

"Who needs a bus?" quacked the Duck.
"We've got a Policedog to fly us home!"

The Cat and the Squirrel were happy.
They had their salt for the Pumpkin Soup.
As for the Duck, he had his packet of pepper.
He held it tightly all the way back.

Home again, in the old white cabin.
Pumpkin Soup in the cooking pot.

Made by the Cat who slices up the pumpkin,
made by the Squirrel who stirs in the water,
made by the Duck who tips in a pipkin of salt . . . and . . .

a pipkin of pepper.

Oh no . . .

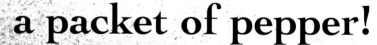

a packet of pepper!

Delicious!